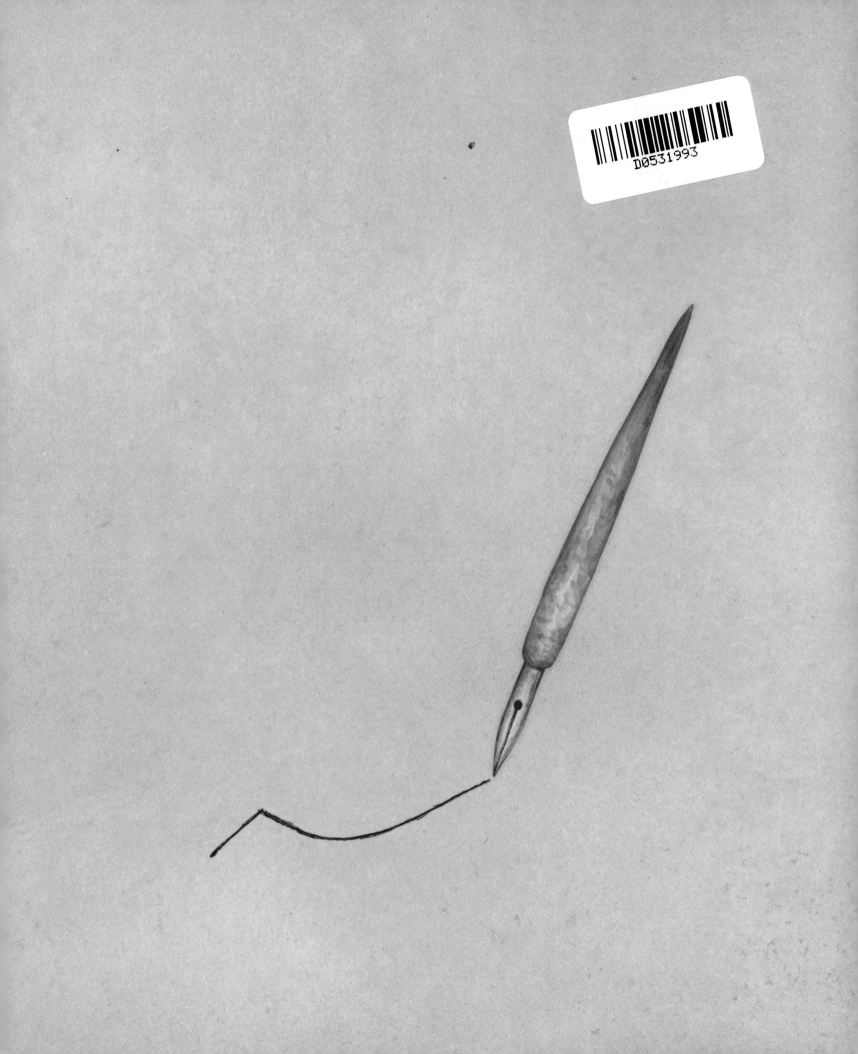

WALLACE EDWARDS

Once Upon a Line

pajamapress

First published in the United States in 2015

Text and illustrations copyright © 2015 Wallace Edwards

This edition copyright © 2015 Pajama Press Inc.

This is a first edition.

10 9 8 7 6 5 4 3 2 1

www.pajamapress.ca   info@pajamapress.ca

The publisher gratefully acknowledges the support of the Canada Council for the Arts and the Ontario Arts Council for its publishing program. We acknowledge the financial support of the Government of Canada through the Canada Book Fund (CBF) for our publishing activities.

Library and Archives Canada Cataloguing in Publication

Edwards, Wallace, author illustrator

     Once upon a line / Wallace Edwards.

ISBN 978-1-927485-78-1 (bound)

     I. Title.

PS8559.D88O53 2015   jC813'.6   C2015-901844-7

Publisher Cataloging-in-Publication Data (U.S.)

Wallace Edwards, 1957

     Once upon a line / Wallace Edwards.

[32] pages : color illustrations ; cm.

Summary: A family discovers a trunk of old paintings by Uncle George, each drawn from a single line using an enchanted pen.

ISBN-13: 978-1927485-78-1

1. Paintings – Juvenile fiction. 2. Magic in art – Juvenile fiction. I. Title

[E] dc23   PZ7.W355On 2015

Original art created with watercolor, pencil, and gouache
Cover and book design by Martin Gould

Manufactured by Sheck Wah Tong Printing Ltd.
Printed in Hong Kong, China

Pajama Press Inc.
181 Carlaw Ave., Suite 207, Toronto, Ontario, Canada, M4M 2S1

Distributed in Canada by UTP Distribution
5201 Dufferin Street, Toronto, Ontario, Canada, M3H 5T8

Distributed in the U.S. by Ingram Publisher Services
1 Ingram Blvd., La Vergne, TN 37086, USA

For Katie, my love.
And for Harriet, Stella, Chase, Miles,
Sage, George, Gordon, Leonie and Jane Freeman

One rainy night many years ago,

we found in the attic a leather folder inside an old steamer trunk. The contents belonged to our Great-Uncle George. Not much is known about him except that he was a magician who traveled the world and disappeared on stage along with a monkey and a motorcycle.

It was said that Great-Uncle George had an enchanted pen from the East. With this pen he would draw an ordinary line. That line turned into a painting. He drew the line many times and painted hundreds of paintings, but all that remain are the ones you see in this book.

Each picture starts with the same pen line. See if you can find it. Each painting is the beginning of a story, and every story begins with "Once upon a line."

Now, use your imagination to finish each story.

ONCE UPON A LINE,
a humble creature made a grand entrance.
"I always decorate my home," she said.
"It helps me remember..."

ONCE UPON A LINE,
there was a great race.
No one knew who would come first
until the fluffy one began to...

ONCE UPON A LINE,
there was a greedy monkey.
One day he realized...

ONCE UPON A LINE,
a fisherman tried out his new fishing pole.
He was admiring the fine workmanship
when suddenly...

ONCE UPON A LINE,
an explorer found a path to a new and strange planet.
Should she stop to explore or keep going?
She finally decided to...

ONCE UPON A LINE,
Mr. Wolf was about to give up searching
for his pet duck when...

ONCE UPON A LINE,
a mermaid found a mysterious object.
She thought that it might be...

ONCE UPON A LINE,
there was a funny duck.
He liked to make alligators laugh because...

ONCE UPON A LINE,
there was a prince who could dream in color.
One night he dreamed of a dragon named...

ONCE UPON A LINE,
a young bird did not want to grow up.
One day while strolling along,
he thought he heard...

ONCE UPON A LINE,
there was a man with a singing shoe.
One night on stage he felt his other shoe
begin to...

ONCE UPON A LINE,
there was a woodpecker with an artistic streak.
One day he thought he heard his tree
begin to...

ONCE UPON A LINE,
there was a reluctant circus performer.
He was tired of getting stuck in a hoop,
and feathers made him sneeze, so he decided to...

ONCE UPON A LINE,
there was a mysterious disappearance.
The only witness said...

ONCE UPON A LINE,
a dandy rat showed off his brand new
ultra-modern house. "I have never had such a beautiful
home before," he said. Just then, a little bird said...

ONCE UPON A LINE,
a figure skater found the formula.
"If you want to have fun," he said,
"all you have to do is..."

ONCE UPON A LINE,
there was a knight who was allergic to horses.
This was not a problem because...

ONCE UPON A LINE,
Captain Kurd grew eager to sight land.
If he didn't find land soon,
he was going to have to...

ONCE UPON A LINE,
there was a moose who played the violin.
He preferred to write his own music because...

ONCE UPON A LINE,
a dog thought she was a cat. But why did she
make barking noises and ignore mice?
One day she suddenly noticed...

ONCE UPON A LINE,
a king enjoyed sorting through
his favorite royal balloons when...

ONCE UPON A LINE,
a penguin grew tired of looking like everyone else.
Whenever he put on his favorite outfit,
the other penguins...

ONCE UPON A LINE,
there was a duck who did not like to get wet.
He was afraid that...

ONCE UPON A LINE,
it finally started to rain.
It was time to...

ONCE UPON A LINE,
it finally stopped raining.
It was then that the seagull told an amazing story.

Thank you
for finding my pen!

The End

Here you'll find the storylines: